MINERVA LOUISE

by Janet Morgan Stoeke

PUFFIN BOOKS

PUFFIN BOOKS
Published by the Penguin Group
Penguin Putnam Books for Young Readers, 345 Hudson Street, New York, New York 10014, U.S.A.
Penguin Books Ltd, 27 Wrights Lane, London W8 5TZ, England
Penguin Books Australia Ltd, Ringwood, Victoria, Australia
Penguin Books Canada Ltd, 10 Alcorn Avenue, Toronto, Ontario, Canada M4V 3B2
Penguin Books (N.Z.) Ltd, 182-190 Wairau Road, Auckland 10, New Zealand

Penguin Books Ltd, Registered Offices: Harmondsworth, Middlesex, England

First published in the United States of America by E. P. Dutton, a division of NAL Penguin Inc., 1988
First published in Puffin Books, 1993
Reissued 2001

1 3 5 7 9 10 8 6 4 2

THE LIBRARY OF CONGRESS HAS CATALOGED THE DUTTON EDITION AS FOLLOWS:
Stoeke, Janet Morgan.
Minerva Louise.
Summary: A hen has fun exploring the house with the red curtains.
[1. Chickens—Fiction. 2. Dwellings—Fiction.]
I. Title.
PZ7.S8696Mi 1988 [E] 87-24458
ISBN 0-525-44374-6

This edition ISBN 0-14-056811-5

Printed in the United States of America

for Paul, David and Sarah

Minerva Louise loved the house

with the red curtains.

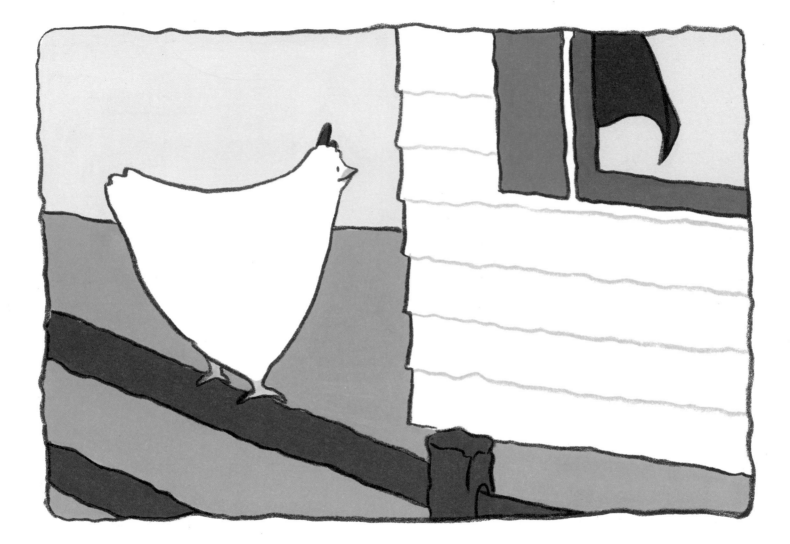

I wonder, she said,

what could this be?

Maybe a new place for me!

Look, here's the perfect nest...

a comfortable chair...

and friendly cows.

Even a tractor!

A meadow of flowers. . . .

tasty foods…all kinds of things!

Except there's no one here
to play with.

But that can't be.

It's such a wonderful place!

Someone must be here.

Oh! Who are you?
Will you play with me?

No, not in that big puddle!

I like to play in the yard
with my friends. Look!

There they are! I'm going out
to play now, but I'll be back.

And Minerva Louise did come back,

because she loved the house
with the red curtains.